A ROBOT NAMED CHIP

PHILIPPE DUPASQUIER

Andersen Press · London

CW01604190

For Klaus

Copyright ©1990 by Philippe Dupasquier.
This paperback edition first published in 2001 by Andersen Press Ltd.
The rights of Philippe Dupasquier to be identified as the author and illustrator of this work have been asserted by him in accordance with the Copyright, Designs and Patents Act, 1988.
First published in Great Britain in 1990 by Andersen Press Ltd., 20 Vauxhall Bridge Road, London SW1V 2SA. Published in Australia by Random House Australia Pty., 20 Alfred Street, Milsons Point, Sydney, NSW 2061.All rights reserved. Colour separated in Switzerland by Photolitho AG, Zurich. Printed and bound in China.

10 9 8 7 6 5 4 3 2 1

British Library Cataloguing in Publication Data available.

ISBN 0 86264 266 3

This book has been printed on acid-free paper

On the planet Adelaide, in the city of Alpha 4, Mrs Baines was finishing off her lesson with class 2 . . .

"Alpha 4 is built on five levels and is Adelaide's most important city."
BEEP! BEEP! BEEP! went the alarm for the end of school.
"That will be all for today," concluded Mrs Baines.

"Good!" thought Peter. "Now I can get back to building my robot."
"Don't forget your maths exercise on Monday!" called Mrs Baines.

On his way home, Peter walked past the robot shop. He remembered when his own robot had first arrived — in a big star-shaped kit — on his birthday. Peter had called him Chip because he was all in pieces.

Chip was only a simple robot. He wouldn't be able to talk. He wouldn't be able to think. All he would be able to do was move around. But Peter was very proud of him all the same.

As soon as he was home, Peter rushed to his room and started to work on his robot. It was almost finished now. That evening Peter's father, Professor Spencer, came to help.
"You've done a great job, Peter," said Professor Spencer, "but I am afraid there is a small piece of the memory missing."

Peter searched everywhere, but couldn't find it.
"Perhaps you'd better come to the laboratory with me tomorrow," said his father, "to see if we can find one."
Peter tingled from the tips of his toes. Professor Spencer worked on Level 5. It was the most secret part of the planet and Peter had never been there before. He dreamt about it all night long.

The next day Peter and his father caught the space bus and went deep into the city to Level 5.
In the laboratory Peter met the rest of his father's team, while Professor Spencer searched everywhere for a part to fit Peter's robot. But try as he might, he couldn't find one.

“I am afraid we will have to use a different memory,” said the Professor. “This one is really for a far more intelligent robot, but if we plug Chip into the Transplant Machine, I am sure it will do the trick.”

The Transplant Machine looked like a giant operating table with huge mechanical arms. Peter gulped. All of a sudden he felt very nervous. The machine clanked and whirred and hissed and fizzed, until at last the robot was finished.

Peter held his breath . . .
For a moment nothing happened.
Then very slowly the robot sat up.

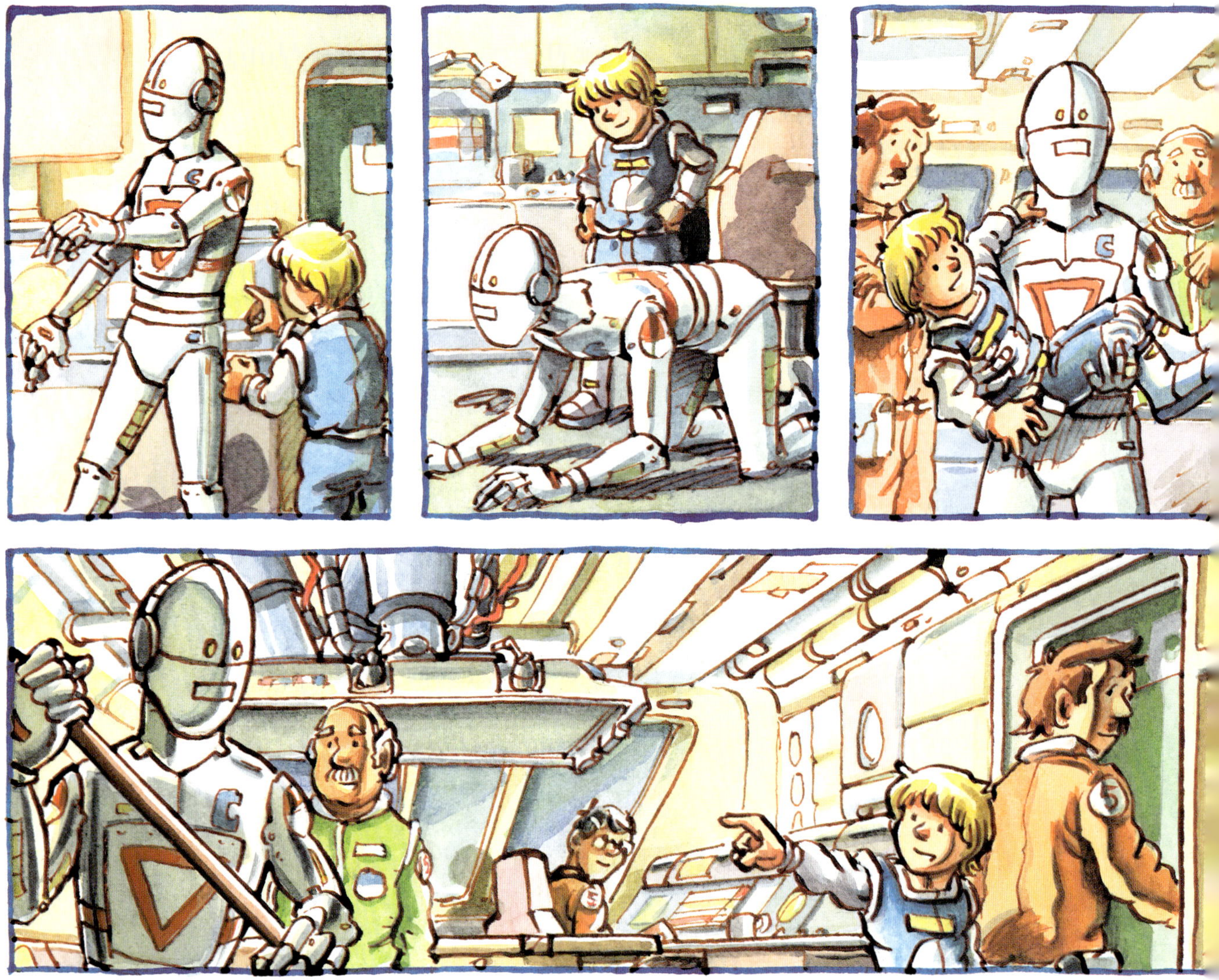

"Stand!" said Peter and the robot stood up.
"Kneel!" said Peter and the robot knelt down.
"Carry me!" said Peter and the robot carried him across the room.
Everybody clapped and cheered.
"Now why don't you find something for the robot to do?"
suggested Professor Spencer. "Then we can see the rest of Level 5."
So Peter gave Chip a broom and told him to sweep the floor.

Outside the laboratory, Peter and Professor Spencer stepped into the airmobile. Peter shivered with excitement as they set off. "This is one of the space shuttles," his father explained.

Peter's eyes grew wide as wheels, as the airmobile sped on and on, through the launch pad and past gleaming rockets . . .

. . . then into the control deck, where the universe rolled past on an enormous screen.

Further and further they went and Peter saw things he would never before have dreamed possible.
Finally, they returned to the laboratory.
"Chip! Chip!" called Peter as he rushed inside. But to his surprise, the robot had disappeared.

The Professor scratched his head. “Where can he be?” he asked.
Everybody looked around.
“There! He’s there!” shouted Peter, peering through a large glass panel.
The Professor gasped in horror. “He’s in the Great Maze!” he cried.

"What's the Great Maze?" asked Peter.
"We call it the Brain of Alpha 4," replied his father, "because without it, nothing would work! Let's just hope Chip doesn't touch anything."

Quick as a flash, Professor Spencer raised the alarm and everybody zoomed down the chute.
Peter and his father put on some special suits and entered the Great Maze.

Inside, everything was quiet and rather eerie. Peter and his father moved anxiously through the Great Maze. Ahead of them they could just see Chip. He had dropped the broom on the floor.
"Chip!" commanded Peter. "Come here!"
The robot turned and started to walk towards him. But suddenly, he tripped . . .

There was a blinding flash, followed by a terrific boom. Then everything went silent again.
Peter and Professor Spencer rushed over to where Chip lay lifeless on the floor. His head had been badly damaged. They carried him out of the maze.

"How did he get in?" asked Peter, as a large tear rolled down his cheek.
"The guard must have thought he belonged to Level 5," replied his father. "He's very similar to the other robots we use here."
"It's all right," called one of the men. "There's no damage to the system. Everything's working OK."
But Peter didn't hear him. He just turned sadly away.

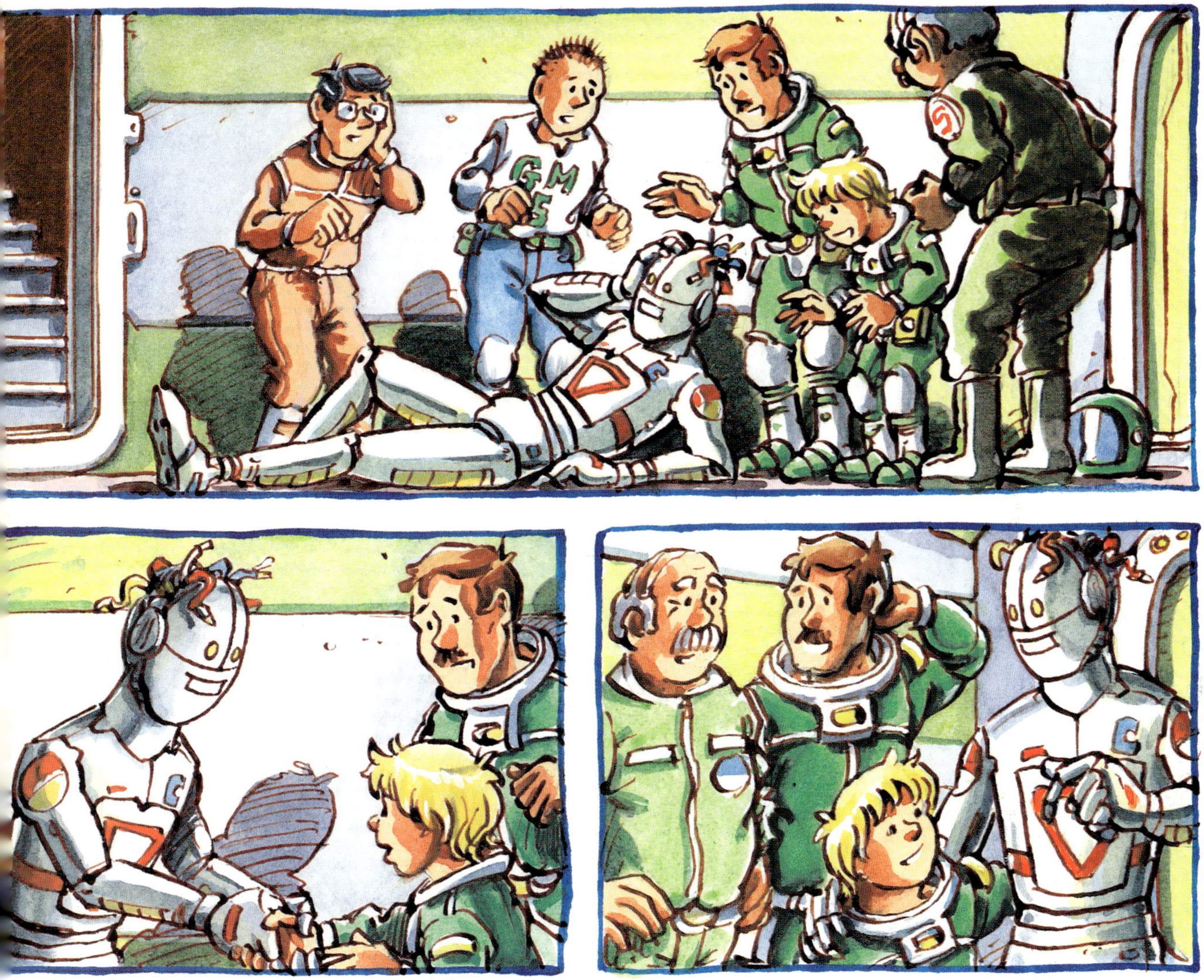

"What a shock! What a shock!" said a loud unfamiliar voice.
Peter spun around. He couldn't believe his eyes. There was the robot — sitting up and rubbing his head!
"So pleased to meet you!" said Chip, holding out his hand to Peter.
"Extraordinary!" said the Professor. "And he can actually talk! The shock must have activated that new memory we fitted him with."

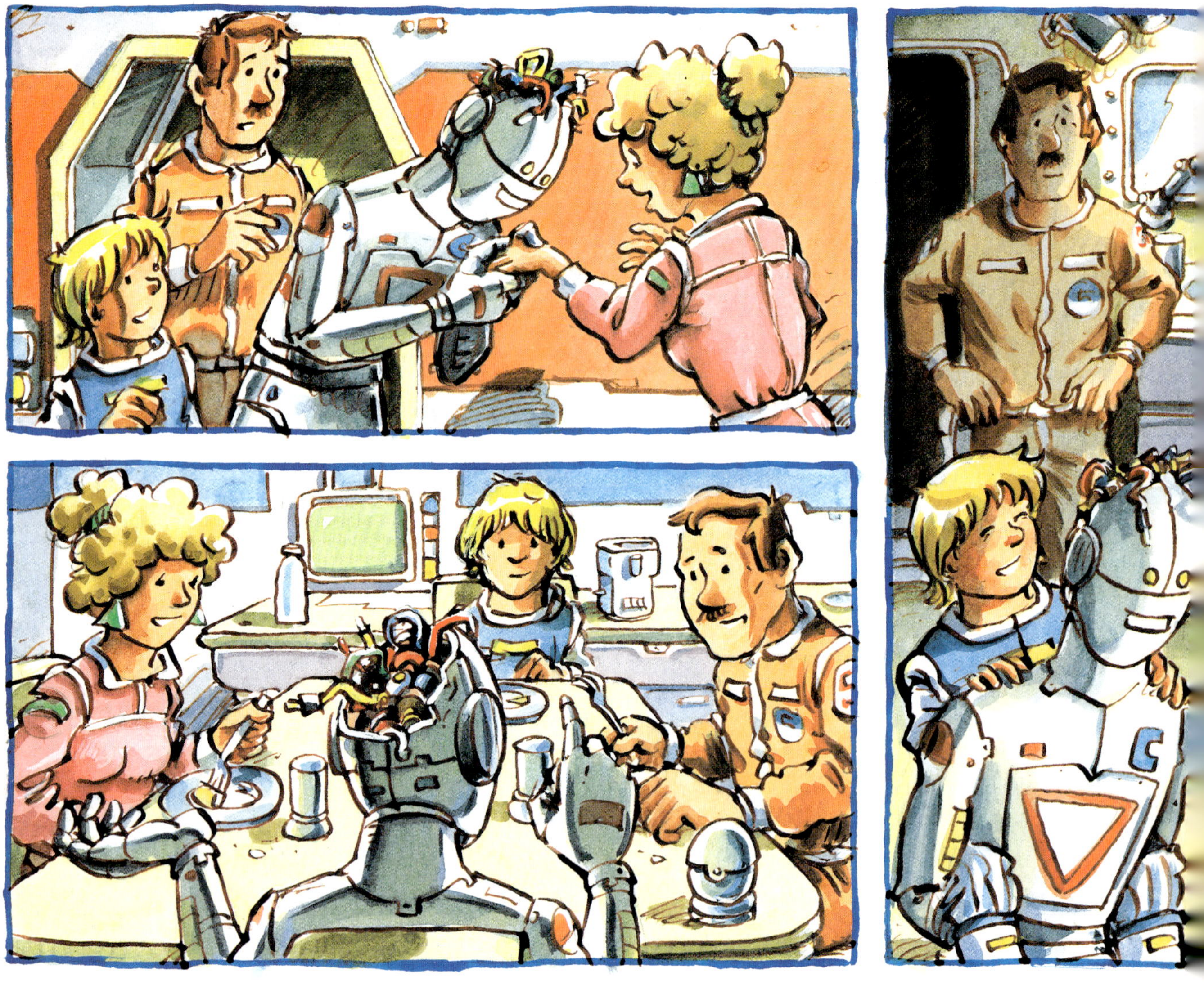

Back home, Peter was having a wonderful time. Not only was Chip amazingly clever, he could also think up the most brilliant games.

So it wasn't until Sunday evening, when it was time to go to bed, that Peter remembered about his maths exercise for school . . .

The next day, Peter took Chip into Class 2. Everyone was very impressed.
"What a clever robot!" said Mrs Baines, as she handed back Peter's maths exercise.

"And your work is unusually good, Peter. Did you do it all by yourself?"

Peter nodded guiltily.

"Then perhaps tomorrow you would like to show us all how . . ." smiled Mrs Baines.

And when Peter rushed home that evening, it wasn't to play with his robot — it was to work on his maths instead!